SAYINGS

●

The Wisdom of Zen

Edited by Manuela Dunn Mascetti
Introduction by T. H. Barrett

HYPERION

NEW YORK

For information address:
Hyperion, 114 Fifth Avenue, New York, NY 10011

ISBN 0-7868-6253-X

Designed by Gautier Design, London
Image selection by Timeless Enterprise (UK) Ltd., London

Library of Congress Cataloging-in-Publication Data
Sayings: the wisdom of Zen / edited by Manuela Dunn; introduction by
    T.H. Barrett. — [1st ed.]
    p.   cm. — (A Box of Zen)
    ISBN 0-7868-6253-X
    1. Zen Buddhism. I. Dunn, Manuela, 1965– . II. Barrett, Timothy Hugh. III. Series.
BQ9265.4.S29 1996
294.3'443—dc20   96–33725
                                                                      CIP

Printed and bound in the United States of America by Quebecor-Kingsport
FIRST EDITION
10 9 8 7 6 5 4 3 2 1

CONTENTS

INTRODUCTION

Zen doubts over the value of writing would at first glance seem to be betrayed by the book you are reading now. Why more words, when verbiage obscures enlightenment like an entanglement of creepers smothering a living plant? But the true Zen master finds an equal obscurantism in silence: in the cause of enlightenment, the terse but telling phrase, compact enough to strike a spark, far outweighs any amount of dead letters or dumb silence. In Zen's Golden Age it was usually a fragment of living speech that set minds ablaze with a light that has shone through the centuries: that is why Zen sayings were valued then, and why they are valued now.

What strikes hardest and fastest is the simple utterance, as pared down as a line of poetry, and indeed one later writer observed that many Zen sayings constitute lines of poetry. No wonder then, that there are traces in early sources of the circulation of Zen anecdotes by word of mouth; like all outstanding communicators the Zen masters are best remembered (like the great wits of our own century) for

6

their most pungent remarks; the spontaneity of religious insight in an age of doubt and despair would have struck home with particular force. For though the backdrop to the meeting described here of Yakusan and Rikoh—Yao-shan and Li Ao, in the Chinese pronunciation—is conventionally painted as one of rustic tranquillity, in reality the countryside harbored bandits or warlord soldiers, while the cities, too, had their gangs of hooligans. Immediate access to the truth was an urgent matter.

So transcripts of the masters' sayings, bristling as they were with colloquialisms shunned in polite literature, came to be esteemed as "Recorded Sayings," abiding reflections of their

living presence. Whether Yao-shan and Li Ao have been reported verbatim I cannot say—the subtle interplay of character and dialogue suggests to me, at any rate, that their story has acquired a certain polish in being passed from hand to hand. Yet the Zen preference for commemorating the everyday and colloquial is clearly there from the start, and affects even later figures like Ta Hui who, while communicating in writing to his followers, retains a directness that speaks to us even today. For he, too, inhabited no idealized, misty landscape, but a world of sorrow and pain like our own, and many of his remarks confront directly death and loss in his community.

While some of these sayings are well over a thousand years old, there is no trace of the quaint or remote about them: rather our modern discourse seems trite and superficial by comparison. Whether these sayings convey enlightenment to us or not, they may at least teach us humility before the men and women of the past. What we do and say will surely be all but forgotten in a hundred—let alone a thousand—years, but here are words, plain words, that have stood the test of time.

T. H. Barrett
Professor of East Asian History
School of African and Oriental Studies
University of London

ZEN LINES

Zen traces a unique lineage of enlightenment directly from Buddha. According to legend, the birth of the understanding of what was to become Zen occurred at a single moment of great significance in one of Buddha's discourses, "The Sermon on the Mount of the Holy Vulture." Buddha was preaching to a gathering of his disciples. He sat upon the podium and remained completely silent for a long time, and, instead of resorting to words in order to explain his point that day, he lifted a single lotus flower and held it in his hand for all to see. The disciples were baffled and could not understand the significance of his gesture, except for Mahakashyapa who quietly smiled at Buddha to show that he fully grasped the meaning of his gesture. Buddha, seeing his smile, declared, "I have the most precious treasure, spiritual and transcendental, which this moment I hand over to you, O venerable Mahakashyapa." Bodhidharma, who brought Zen Buddhism to China, was a direct spiritual descendant of Mahakashyapa.

Zen followers generally agree that this incident is the origin of their doctrine, for by raising the flower, Buddha symbolically revealed the innermost mind of Buddha-nature. The essence of Zen is revealed in what happened to Mahakashyapa, who, by letting the silence of the master penetrate to the very core of his being, understood its deep significance and attained enlightenment. The master is silent, the disciple smiles, the two minds are one. For the nearly two-and-a-half millennia that date the history of Zen, enlightenment has been the way of transmitting the message from one generation of Zen monks to the next. This direct line of experience resembles a transmission of the lamp that was first lit by Buddha so many centuries before. The sayings of the masters are thus an invaluable recording of wisdom traced through the centuries, wisdom that is as timeless as it is poignant and pertinent to us today.

Zen stories are known as *sutras*, a word initially used for the sermons of
Buddha, but later also applied to the words exchanged between Zen masters
and their disciples. Zen sutras present vivid pictures of the unimaginably vast,
multilevel, intercommunicating reality experienced by the enlightened. The

whole enterprise of the teaching and attainment of enlightenment is shown taking place in countless ways and among all manner of beings. The ordinary barriers of time, space, self, and other are transcended in these accounts of visionaries of the past. Zen sutras are perhaps the only existing chronicle, spanning over generations, of enlightened masters speaking. Sutras are a timeless treasure-trove in the extensive literature produced by the Zen school. Unlike the difficult koans, or the contemplative haiku, the sayings and stories of Zen masters are anecdotes of lives, facts, teachings, and events of real-life monks and nuns. As such, they are both ordinary and extraordinary and allow readers to view enlightenment within a down-to-earth context. What transpires from reading these chronicles is that the aim of Zen practitioners was not to escape from the world, but to achieve the kind of detachment and insight that would enable them to become immune to worldly entanglements. At the same time, it would allow them to function in the world with immense compassion, as they strove to bring enlightenment to others.

This book is a commemorative collection of stories, sutras, parables, proverbs, and sayings that run like a clear mountain stream from the past to the present to quench our spiritual thirst and cleanse our minds. One of the things that made Buddha's teachings so radical was his emphasis upon personal experience. In his sermons, Buddha repeatedly encouraged people to "come and see" for themselves, not to rely on scriptures, beliefs, or faith. Thus Zen developed its own unique contours and a set of beautifully tailored techniques for use in obtaining a direct experience of one's true nature—*satori* ("enlightenment" in Japanese).

Delightful, challenging, mystifying, mind-stopping, outrageous, and often scandalous, Zen is today the same soul-intriguing and totality-awakening experience as it was when Buddha reached enlightenment under the Bodhi tree. Zen has been a civilizing influence in Southeast Asia for centuries, and today it enriches and brings meaning to millions of lives, not only in Japan and Korea, but more and more to Western seekers who find sanctuary in the religion's simplicity and immediacy. At its core Zen is a diamond-hard way of attaining *religiousness* that has withstood the test of centuries and goes on shedding fragranced petals wherever it is established.

REFLECTIONS OF
a ZEN MASTER

ON MINDLESSNESS

An 'ancient worthy had a saying: "To look for the ox, one must seek out its tracks. To study the path, seek out mindlessness. Where the tracks are, so must the ox be." The path of mindlessness is easy to seek out. So-called mindlessness is not being inert and unknowing like earth, wood, tile, or stone; it means that the mind is settled and imperturbable when in contact with situations and meeting circumstances; that it does not cling to anything, but is clear in all places, without hindrance or obstruction; without being stained, yet without dwelling in the stainlessness; viewing body and mind like dreams or illusions, yet without remaining in the perspective of dreams' and illusions' empty nothingness.

Only when one arrives at a realm like this, can it be called true mindlessness. . . .

"Just get to the root, don't worry about the branches."

Emptying this mind is the root. Once you get the root, the fundamental, then all kinds of language and knowledge and all your daily activities as you respond to people and adapt to circumstances, through so many upsets and downfalls, whether joyous or angry, good or bad, favorable or adverse—these are all trivial matters, the branches. If you can be spontaneously aware and knowing as you are going along with circumstances, then there is neither lack nor excess.

TA HUI IN A LETTER TO HUNG PO-CH'ENG

TEND THE OX

Since you are studying this path, then at all times in your encounters with people and responses to circumstances you must not let wrong thoughts continue. If you cannot see through them, then the moment a wrong thought comes up you should quickly concentrate your mental energy to pull yourself away. If you always follow these thoughts and let them continue without a break, not only does this obstruct the path, but it makes you out to be a man without wisdom.

In the old days Kuei Shan asked Lazy An, "What work do you do during the twenty-four hours of the day?"

An said, "I tend an ox."

Kuei Shan said, "How do you tend it?"

An said, "Whenever it gets into the grass, I pull it back by the nose."

Kuei Shan said, "You are really tending the ox!"

People who study the path, in controlling their thoughts, should be like Lazy An tending his ox; then gradually a wholesome ripening will take place of itself.

TA HUI

THE INESCAPABLE

Whenever you run into something inescapable amidst the hubbub, you've been examining yourself constantly, but without applying the effort to meditate. This very inescapability itself is meditation: if you go further and adapt and apply effort to examine yourself, you're even further away.

Right when you're in something inescapable, do not bestir your mind and think of examining yourself. The patriarch said, "When discrimination doesn't arise, the light of emptiness shines by itself." Again, Layman P'ang said:

> In daily activities without discrimination,
> I alone naturally harmonize.
> Not grasping or rejecting anywhere,
> Not going with or going against.
> Who considers crimson and purple honorable?
> There's not a spec of dust in the mountains.
> Spiritual powers and wondrous functioning:
> Hauling water and carrying firewood.
> Just when you can't escape, suddenly you get rid of the cloth bag (of illusion) and
> without being aware of it you will be clapping your hands and laughing loudly.

Ta Hui

DISCRIMINATING CONSCIOUSNESS AND WISDOM

Constantly calculating and making plans, flowing along with birth and death, becoming afraid and agitated—all these are sentiments of discriminating consciousness. Yet people studying the path these days do not recognize this disease, and just appear and disappear in its midst. In the teachings it's called acting according to discriminating consciousness, not according to wisdom. Thereby they obscure the scenery of the fundamental ground, their original face. But if you can abandon it all at once, so you neither think nor calculate, then these very sentiments of discriminating consciousness are the subtle wisdom of true emptiness—there is no other wisdom that can be attained. . . .

This subtle wisdom of the true emptiness is coeval with the great void: the void is not subject to being obstructed by things, nor does it hinder the coming and going of all things within it.

TA HUI

THE SAYINGS OF
LAYMAN P'ANG

P'ang Yun was born in China in 740 and died in 808. Although he was a poor and simple man, he attained enlightenment as an ardent follower of *Ch'an* ("Zen" in Chinese). His timeless wisdom shows us that Zen is not a cloistered virtue cultivated by a few monks in remote monasteries, far and away from the daily toils of ordinary humanity. Zen is serenity and peace in every moment and action, and it is an open invitation to everyone. Layman P'ang, as he was known, was greatly admired by the Chinese, and even today his stories are used as teachings in many Zen schools.

Layman P'ang visited the great master Shih-t'ou to find out about Ch'an. One day Shih-t'ou said to the Layman: "Since seeing me, what have your daily activities been?"

"When you ask me about my daily activities, I can't open my mouth," the Layman replied.

"Just because I know you are thus I now ask you," said Shih-t'ou. Whereupon the Layman offered this verse:

> *My daily activities are not unusual,*
> *I'm just naturally in harmony with them.*
> *Grasping nothing, discarding nothing,*
> *In every place, there's no hindrance, no conflict.*

Who assigns the ranks of vermilion and purple?—
The hills' and mountains' last speck of dust is extinguished.
Supernatural power and marvelous activity—
Drawing water and carrying firewood.

Shih-t'ou gave his assent. Then he asked: "Will you put on black robes
or will you continue wearing white?"
"I want to do what I like," replied the Layman.
So he did not shave his head or dye his clothing.
As the Layman and Sung-shan were walking together one day
they saw a group of monks picking greens.
"The yellow leaves are discarded, the green leaves are kept," said Sung-shan.
"How about not falling into green or yellow?" asked the Layman.
"Better you tell me," said Sung-shan.
"For the two of us to be host and guest is most difficult," returned the Layman.
"Yet having come here, you strain to make yourself ruler!" said Sung-shan.
"Who doesn't!" retorted the Layman.
"True, true," agreed Sung-shan.
"To speak about 'not falling into green or yellow' is especially difficult,"
said the Layman.

"But you just did so," returned Sung-shan, laughing.
"Take care of yourselves," called the Layman to the group of monks.
"The monks forgive you for falling into activity," said Sung-shan.
At that the Layman went off.

The Layman was once lying on his couch reading a sutra. A monk saw him
and said, "Layman! You must maintain dignity while reading a sutra."
The Layman raised up one leg.
The monk had nothing to say.

Not wanting to discard greed and anger,
In vain you trouble to read Buddha's teachings.
You see the prescription, but don't take the medicine—
How then can you do away with your illness!
Grasp emptiness, and emptiness is form;
Grasp form, and form is impermanent.
Emptiness and form are not mine—
Sitting erect, I see my native home.

Zen Anecdotes

NIGHT RAIN

*B*efore he went to live in the mountains, Zen master Ranryo traveled throughout the four quarters, making no distinction between court and countryside, city and village, not avoiding even wineshops and brothels. When someone asked him why he acted in this way, the Zen master said,

"My Way is right there, wherever I happen to be. There is no gap at all."

Later Ranryo went into the mountains, where he built a simple hut and lived a life of frugal austerity as he continued to work on Zen.

Especially fond of night rain, Ranryo would burn incense and sit up on rainy nights, even until dawn. The people of the mountain villages, not knowing his name, used to call him "the Night Rain Monk." This amused him, so he began to use Night Rain as a literary name.

Once a visitor asked Ranryo about the relative merits of Zen meditation and the Pure Land Buddhist practice of Buddha-remembrance, reciting the name of the Buddha of Infinite Light. Ranryo gave his answer in verse:

> *Zen meditation and Buddha-remembrance*
> *are like two mountains;*
> *Higher and lower potentials*
> *divide a single world.*
> *When they arrive, all alike*
> *see the moon atop the peak;*
> *only pity those who have no faith*
> *and suffer over the climb.*

SOMETHING FROM NOTHING

Once on a journey Zen master Zenko happened to see a ruined temple that he thought should be restored. Completely without material resources of his own, Zenko wrote a large sign saying, "This month, on such-and-such a day, the pilgrim Zen master Zenko will perform a self-cremation. Let those who will donate money for firewood come watch."

Now Zenko posted this sign here and there. Soon the local people were agog, and donations began pouring in.

On the appointed day, people jammed the temple, awaiting the lighting of the fire. Zenko sat in the firewood, preparing to immolate himself. He called for the fuel to be ignited at his signal.

Now Zenko went into silent meditation. A long time passed. All of a sudden, he looked up at the sky and nodded. Then he addressed the crowd, saying, "Listen, listen! There are voices in the clouds! Just as I was about to enter into extinction, the saints all said, 'It is still too early for you to think of leaving the defiled world! Put up with this world for a while, and stay here to save living beings.' So I can't go on with the cremation today."

Then he took the money that had been donated and was able to restore the abandoned temple with it.

THE ELEVENTH HOUR

*C*hosha used to come to participate in the special annual intensive meditation session with Zen master Hakuin every single year, yet he never attained anything.

Finally one year Hakuin said to him at the conclusion of the session: "You come here every year, just like a duck diving into the water when it is cold. You are making a long journey in vain, without gaining half a bit of empowerment. I can't imagine how many straw sandals you have worn out over the years making this trip. I have no use for idlers like you around here, so don't come anymore!"

Deeply stirred, Chosha thought to

himself, "Am I not a man? If I do not penetrate through to realization this time,
I will never return home alive. I will concentrate on meditation until I die."
Setting himself a limit of seven days, Chosha went to sit in a fishnet shed by the
seashore. But even after seven days of sitting in meditation without eating or sleeping,
Chosha was still at a loss. There was nothing for him to do but drown himself
in the ocean. Removing his shoes in the traditional manner of a suicide rite,
Chosha stood in the waves. At that moment, seeing the shimmering ocean and
the rising sun merging into a crimson radiance, all at once he became completely
empty and greatly awakened.

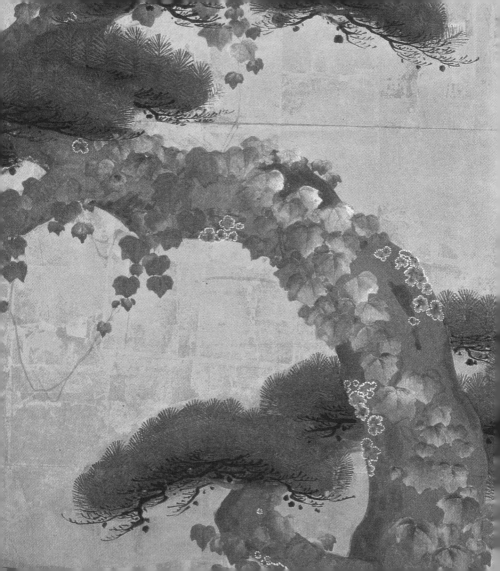

Zen Sutras

Yakusan had not given a discourse for some time when, one day, the head monk came and said, "The congregation of monks are thinking about you preaching a sermon." Yakusan said, "Ring the bell!" The superior rang the bell, but when all the monks gathered, Yakusan went back to his room. The head monk followed him and said, "The master was going to give a talk, and the monks are all ready; why didn't you say anything to them?" Yakusan said, "There are sutra priests for the sutras, shastra priests for the shastras; why do you question my goings-on?"

Yakusan (751–834) became a priest at the age of seventeen and succeeded Sekito, becoming an outstanding Zen master. He established a monastery of great repute. He is one of the teachers mentioned in *The Blue Cliff Records*. This sutra shows the subtlety of Yakusan's teaching: although he agreed to give a talk, the talk itself was never given. That which needs to be said cannot be said, truth is a silent transmission. Yakusan deemed his monks mature enough to understand that sutra and shastra priests could expound on the dharma, but that the ultimate teaching has nothing to do with words.

In the days when Yakusan was still actively instructing his disciples, Rikoh—the governor of Ho-shu and also a great Confucian—went to visit

Yakusan, whom he greatly admired.
Yakusan was looking at a sutra when
the attendant monk showed Rikoh into
the master's room. Yakusan did not look up
at the governor's arrival, but he appeared
absorbed in what he was reading.
After a few moments, Rikoh, who had a
hot temper, could not stand it anymore.
He grumbled, "It's better to hear your
name than to see your face," and stood
up to leave.
Immediately Yakusan said, "Why do you
respect the ear and look down on the eye?"
Rikoh pressed his hands together and
bowed down. He then asked, "Could you
please tell me what the Tao is?"
Yakusan immediately pointed up and
then down with his hand and asked,
"Do you understand?"
Rikoh said, "I don't understand."

Yakusan shouted, "Clouds are in the sky; water is in the well!"

Rikoh suddenly realized and felt great joy. And with his contentment, he bowed down to Yakusan and presented this poem to him:

> Achieved form, it looks like a form of the crane.
>
> Under the thousands of pine trees, the way of the two poles.
>
> I come and ask Tao: no wasteful argument.
>
> Clouds are in the sky; water is in the well.

One day, Tanka [Tennen] said to the monks who were with him, "You should all protect your essential thing, which is not made or formed by you. So how can I teach you to do this or not to do this?

Once, when I saw Sekito Osho, he taught me that I should just protect it by myself. This thing cannot be talked about. You all have your own zazen mat; other than that, what Zen do you talk about?

You should understand this. There is nothing which is to become Buddha. Don't just go on hearing the name of Buddha; you, yourselves, must see that the good devices and four infinite virtues are not from the outside; don't carry them in your mind.

What do you intend to follow? Don't use sutras.

Leave the emptiness without falling into it.

The seekers of the present day search for the Tao chaotically.

Here in this place, there is no way to learn,
nor any dharma to show. Even a single sip or a single
bite has its own truth.
Don't entertain thoughts and suspicions. In any place,
the thing is present. If you recognize Gautama Buddha,
an ordinary old man is that. You should all see, and
get it, by yourselves. Don't let a blind man lead a mass
of blind people into a fire cave.
If you play a dice game in the dark night, how can you
see the numbers on the dice?"

Gyozan said to Sekishitsu, "Tell me what to believe in
and what to rely on?"
Sekishitsu gestured across the sky above, three times
with his hand, and said, "What do you say about
reading sutras?"
Sekishitsu replied, "All the sutras are out of the question.
Doing things that are given by others is dualism of mind
and matter. And if you are in the dualism of subject and
object, various views arise. But this is blind wisdom, so it

is not yet the Tao. If others don't give you anything, there is not a single thing.
That's why Bodhidharma said, 'Originally, there is not a single thing.' You see,
when a baby comes out of the womb, does he read sutras or not?
At that time, the baby doesn't know whether such a thing as Buddha-nature exists or
not. As he grows up and learns various views, he appears to the world and says,
'I do well and I understand.' But he doesn't know it is rubbish and delusion. Of the
sixteen ways or phases of doing, a baby's way is the best. The time of a baby's gurgle
is compared to a seeker when he leaves the mind of dividing and choosing. That's why
a baby is praised. But if you take this comparison and say, 'The baby is the way,'
people of the present will understand it wrongly."

LIST OF COLOUR PLATES

Front cover-Night rain at Karasaki by Utagawa Hiroshige, (c) *Ota Memorial Museum, Tokyo*

Pages 4-5-enlarged detail from Night rain at Karasaki by Utagawa Hiroshige, (c) *Ota Memorial Museum, Tokyo*

Page 6-Calligraphies, "Koku" (Time) by the Priest Hakuin, (c) *Eisei Bunko Foundation, Tokyo*

Page 7-Calligraphies, "Shibaraku fuzai shinin no gotoshi" (Let your thoughts wander for an instant and you are no better than a dead man) by the Priest Hakuin, (c) *Eisei Bunko Foundation, Tokyo*

Page 8-Calligraphies, "Long life" by the Priest Hakuin, (c) *Eisei Bunko Foundation, Tokyo*

Pages 10-11-(c) *British Museum, London*

Page 13-Water-wheel, bridge and willow-tree in the moonlight, anonymous, (c) *Kyoto National Museum, Kyoto*

Pages 14, 17-(c) *British Museum, London*

Pages 18-19-Quail, millet and foxtail with autumn flowers by Tosa Mitsuoki, (c) *Fukuoka Collection, Kanagawa*

Pages 20, 23, 24, 27-Agriculture in the four seasons by Kusumi Morikage, (c) *Kyoto National Museum, Kyoto*

Pages 28-29, 31, 32, 35, 36-37-(c) *British Museum, London*

Page 38-Fifty-two stages of the Tokkaido by Utagawa Hiroshige, (c) *Tokyo National Museum, Tokyo*

Page 41-detail from One hundred views of Mt. Fuji by Hokusai, (c) *Hiraki Ukiyo-E Museum, Yokohama*

Page 42-Landscape by Tani Buncho, (c) *Tokyo National Museum, Tokyo*

Pages 44-45-detail from Pine-trees in the four seasons by Kano Tan'Yu, *Daitokuji, Kyoto*

Page 47-Bodhidharma in meditation by the Priest Hakuin, (c) *Eisei Bunko Foundation, Tokyo*

Page 48, right and page 48, left-(c) *British Museum, London*

Page 50-Calligraphies, "Chu" (The middle) by the Priest Hakuin, (c) *Eisei Bunko Foundation, Tokyo*

ACKNOWLEDGMENTS

The editors gratefully acknowledge the following sources:

Swampland Flowers-The Letters and Lectures of Zen Master Ta Hui, Cristopher Cleary, Grove Atlantic Inc., New York.

Zen Antics, Thomas Cleary, ed. and trans., Shambhala Publications, Boston and London, 1993.

A Man of Zen-The Recorded Sayings of Layman P'ang, Ruth Fuller Sasaki, Yoshitaka Iriya and Dana Fraser, trans. Weatherhill, New York, 1992.

Cleary, Cristopher. *Swampland Flowers-The Letters and Lectures of Zen Master Ta Hui.* New York: Grove Atlantic Inc.

Cleary, Thomas. *Zen Antics.* Boston and London: Shambhala Publications, 1993.

Sasaki, Ruth Fuller, Yoshitaka Iriya, and Dana Fraser, trans. *A Man of Zen-The Recorded Sayings of Layman P'ang.* New York: Weatherhill, 1992.

Aoyama, Shundo. *Zen Seeds—Reflections of a Female Priest.*
   Tokyo: Kosei Publishing Company, 1990.

Cleary, Christopher.
   Swampland Flowers—The Letters and Lectures of Zen Master Ta Hui.
   New York: Grove Atlantic Inc.

Cleary, J. C., trans. and ed. *A Tune Beyond the Clouds.*
   Berkeley: Asian Humanities Press, 1990.

Cleary, Thomas. *Zen Antics.* Boston and London: Shambhala, 1993.

Osho. *Dogen, the Zen Master: A Search and a Fulfillment.*

———. *Isan: No Footprints in the Sky.*

———. *Joshu: The Lion's Roar.* Poona, India: Osho Foundation International.

———. *Ma Tzu: The Empty Mirror.*

———. *Nansen: The Point of Departure.*

———. *Rinzai: Master of the Irrational.*

———. *Yakusan: Straight to the Point of Enlightenment.*
   Poona, India: Osho Foundation International.

Sasaki, Ruth Fuller, Yoshitaka Iriya, and Dana Fraser, trans.
   A Man of Zen—The Recorded Sayings of Layman P'ang.
   New York: Weatherhill, 1992.

Manuela Dunn Mascetti is the author of *The Song of Eve, Saints, Goddess,* and coauthor with Peter Lorie of *The Quotable Spirit.* A Zen student of many years, she lives in London with her husband and her two Tiffanies named after Zen monks.

Professor Timothy Hugh Barrett, formerly Head of the History Department at the prestigious London School of Oriental and African Studies, is an expert on East Asian History who has studied Zen in both Japan and China for many years.